GREATEST OF ALL TIME
SPORTS STARS

THE GREATEST HOCKEY PLAYERS OF ALL TIME

Gareth Stevens
PUBLISHING

BY ERIC KEPPELER

Please visit our website, www.garethstevens.com. For a free color catalog of all our high-quality books, call toll free 1-800-542-2595 or fax 1-877-542-2596.

Cataloging-in-Publication Data

Names: Keppeler, Eric.
Title: The greatest hockey players of all time / Eric Keppeler.
Description: New York : Gareth Stevens Publishing, 2020. | Series: Greatest of all time: sports stars | Includes glossary and index.
Identifiers: ISBN 9781538247839(pbk.) | ISBN 9781538247853(library bound) | ISBN 9781538247846(6 pack)
Subjects: LCSH: Hockey players–Rating of–Juvenile literature. | Hockey players–Statistics–Juvenile literature. | Hockey players–Biography–Juvenile literature. | Hockey–Records–Juvenile literature. | Hockey–History–Juvenile literature.
Classification: LCC GV847.25 K47 2020 | DDC 796.9620922 B–dc23

First Edition

Published in 2020 by
Gareth Stevens Publishing
111 East 14th Street, Suite 349
New York, NY 10003

Designer: Katelyn E. Reynolds
Editor: Emily Mahoney

Photo credits: Cover, p. 1 Patrick McDermott/NHLI via Getty Images; cover, pp. 1–32 (series art) Dmitry Kostrov/Shutterstock.com; cover, pp. 1–32 (series background) rangizzz/Shutterstock.com; p. 5 Bruce Bennett/Getty Images; pp. 6, 14, 18, 23 Bruce Bennett Studios via Getty Images/Getty Images; pp. 7, 21 (hockey puck graphic) valterZ/Shutterstock.com; pp. 8, 13, 15 Denis Brodeur/NHLI via Getty Images; p. 9 Howard Sochurek/The LIFE Images Collection via Getty Images/Getty Images; pp. 10, 11, 17 Bettmann/Getty Images; pp. 12, 19 B Bennett/Getty Images; p. 20 Richard Schultz/NHLImages; p. 22 Pictorial Parade/Getty Images; p. 24 Sovfoto/Universal Images Group via Getty Images; p. 25 Steve Powell/Getty Images; p. 26 Doug Pensinger/Getty Images; p. 27 Brian Bahr/Getty Images; p. 28 Kiev.Victor/Shutterstock.com; p. 29 Will Newton/Getty Images.

Printed in the United States of America

CPSIA compliance information: Batch #CW20GS: For further information contact Gareth Stevens, New York, New York at 1-800-542-2595.

CONTENTS

WORDS IN THE GLOSSARY APPEAR IN **BOLD** TEXT THE FIRST TIME THEY ARE USED IN THE TEXT.

THE FASTEST GAME ON ICE

Most people agree that the first hockey game was played on March 3, 1875, in Montreal, Canada. Soon, there were many teams, with the National Hockey League officially starting in 1917.

On the surface, it doesn't seem that hard. Using a curved stick, you and your teammates try to shoot a little rubber puck into the other team's net, scoring a goal. Meanwhile, the other team tries to do the same to you. The team with the most goals at the end of the game is the winner. And all this happens while everyone is on ice skates.

Actually, maybe it does sound pretty hard! But hard work, practice, and skill is what makes some players the greatest of all time.

THE STANLEY CUP IS THE TROPHY AWARDED TO THE NHL'S PLAYOFF CHAMPION TEAM EACH YEAR. THE NAME OF EVERYONE ON THE WINNING TEAM IS **INSCRIBED** ON THE TROPHY. THE ST. LOUIS BLUES WON THE CUP IN 2019, THEIR FIRST CHAMPIONSHIP IN TEAM HISTORY!

WHO'S THE GREATEST?

MILLIONS OF PEOPLE IN COUNTRIES AROUND THE WORLD HAVE PLAYED HOCKEY OVER THE LAST 100 YEARS. SO, HOW DO YOU PICK THE GREATEST OF ALL TIME? IS IT THE ONE WHO PLAYED THE MOST GAMES? SCORED THE MOST GOALS? WON THE MOST GAMES OR CHAMPIONSHIPS? THERE ARE MANY WAYS TO CHOOSE THE GREATEST.

THE GREAT ONE

By the numbers, there's one very clear choice for the greatest hockey player of all time. Wayne Gretzky was born January 26, 1961, in Ontario, Canada. He holds or shares 61 NHL records and won four Stanley Cups with the Edmonton Oilers.

Gretzky broke into the NHL as a 19-year-old **rookie** with Edmonton and scored 51 goals in his first season! His nickname was the Great One—and the Hockey Hall of Fame **waived** its usual 3-year waiting period and inducted, or added, him immediately after his **retirement** on April 16, 1999. His number 99 was retired league-wide a year later.

WAYNE GRETZKY STARTED PLAYING FOR THE OILERS IN 1979.

GRETZKY'S GREATEST RECORDS

MOST CAREER POINTS	2,857
MOST CAREER GOALS	894
MOST CAREER ASSISTS	1,963
MOST GOALS IN ONE SEASON	92
MOST POINTS IN ONE SEASON	215
MOST ASSISTS IN ONE SEASON	163
MOST POINTS IN ONE PLAYOFF SEASON	47
MOST CAREER PLAYOFF POINTS	382
MOST 40-GOAL SEASONS	12
MOST 100-POINT SEASONS	15
FEWEST GAMES TO SCORE 50 GOALS	39 GAMES
LONGEST STREAK WITH AT LEAST ONE POINT	51 GAMES

ANYONE CAN BE TRADED

GRETZKY WAS TRADED TO THE LOS ANGELES KINGS AFTER THE 1987-88 SEASON. WHILE HE CONTINUED TO PUT UP GREAT NUMBERS, HE NEVER WON ANOTHER STANLEY CUP. HE WAS TRADED TO ST. LOUIS DURING THE 1995-96 SEASON AND THEN SPENT HIS LAST 3 YEARS WITH THE NEW YORK RANGERS.

MR. HOCKEY

With a nickname like "Mr. Hockey," you know a player must be special! Gordie Howe had scored the most goals in NHL history (801) until Wayne Gretzky broke his record. Starting in 1946, he played 25 seasons with the Detroit Red Wings, leading them to four Stanley Cup championships and seven straight first-place regular season finishes. He retired from the NHL after the 1970-71 season and was immediately inducted into the Hockey Hall of Fame.

That wasn't the end of this career though! In 1979, at age 51, Howe came back to play one more season with his sons, Mark and Marty Howe, with the Hartford Whalers. He died in 2016.

GORDIE HOWE WON THE NHL'S MVP TROPHY SIX TIMES

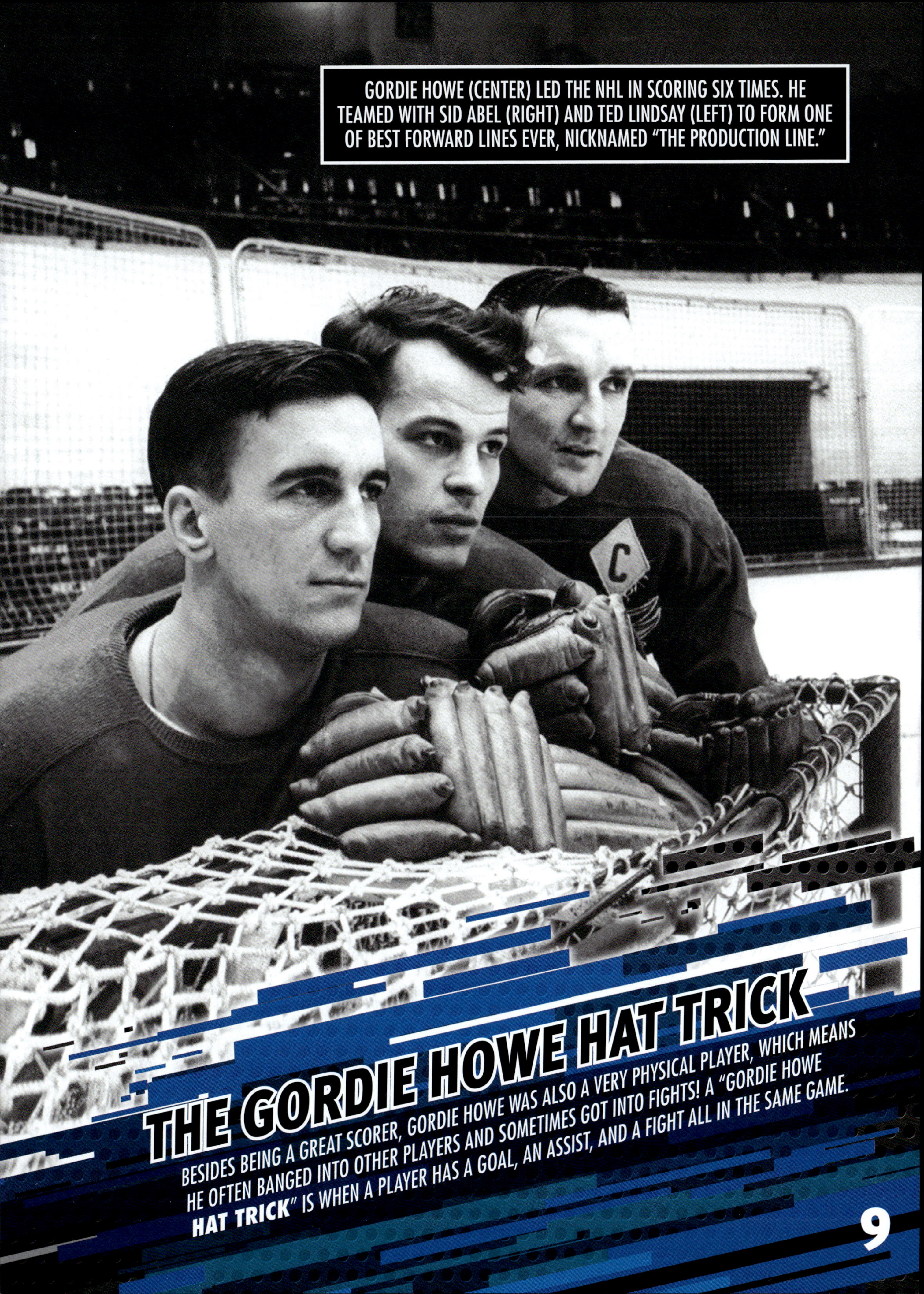

GORDIE HOWE (CENTER) LED THE NHL IN SCORING SIX TIMES. HE TEAMED WITH SID ABEL (RIGHT) AND TED LINDSAY (LEFT) TO FORM ONE OF BEST FORWARD LINES EVER, NICKNAMED "THE PRODUCTION LINE."

THE GORDIE HOWE HAT TRICK

BESIDES BEING A GREAT SCORER, GORDIE HOWE WAS ALSO A VERY PHYSICAL PLAYER, WHICH MEANS HE OFTEN BANGED INTO OTHER PLAYERS AND SOMETIMES GOT INTO FIGHTS! A "GORDIE HOWE **HAT TRICK**" IS WHEN A PLAYER HAS A GOAL, AN ASSIST, AND A FIGHT ALL IN THE SAME GAME.

ROCKET RICHARD

Maurice "Rocket" Richard (rih-SHARD) earned his nickname because of his great speed. Richard played 18 seasons with the Montreal Canadiens, starting in 1942. A 14-time All-Star, he led the Canadiens to eight Stanley Cup titles.

Richard was the first NHL player to score 50 goals in one season. He became the league's all-time leading scorer when he scored his 325th career goal in 1952. He was also the first person to reach 500 career goals, finishing with 544. Today, the NHL trophy for most goals by a player in a season is called the Rocket Richard Trophy.

MAURICE RICHARD OFTEN PLAYED ON A LINE WITH TOE BLAKE AND ELMER LACH, AND THEY BECAME KNOWN AS "THE PUNCH LINE." RICHARD WAS INDUCTED INTO THE HOCKEY HALL OF FAME IN 1961.

TEMPER, TEMPER

THE ROCKET PLAYED ROUGH AND SPENT A LOT OF TIME IN THE **PENALTY** BOX. DURING A FIGHT IN 1955, HE PURPOSELY HURT BOSTON BRUIN HAL LAYCOE WITH HIS STICK AND THEN PUNCHED ONE OF THE OFFICIALS. HE WAS **SUSPENDED** FOR THE REST OF THE SEASON, EVEN THOUGH HE WAS LEADING THE LEAGUE IN SCORING!

SUPER MARIO

Mario Lemieux was **drafted** first overall by the Pittsburgh Penguins in 1984. He battled through many health problems to become one of the greatest goal scorers in NHL history.

Lemieux had to retire in 1997 because of Hodgkin's disease, a kind of **cancer**. He was able to start playing again 3 years later but retired for good in 2006 because of heart problems. In parts of 17 seasons, he led the Penguins to two Stanley Cups and scored 690 career goals to reach 10th on the all-time list. He later created the Mario Lemieux **Foundation** for cancer research.

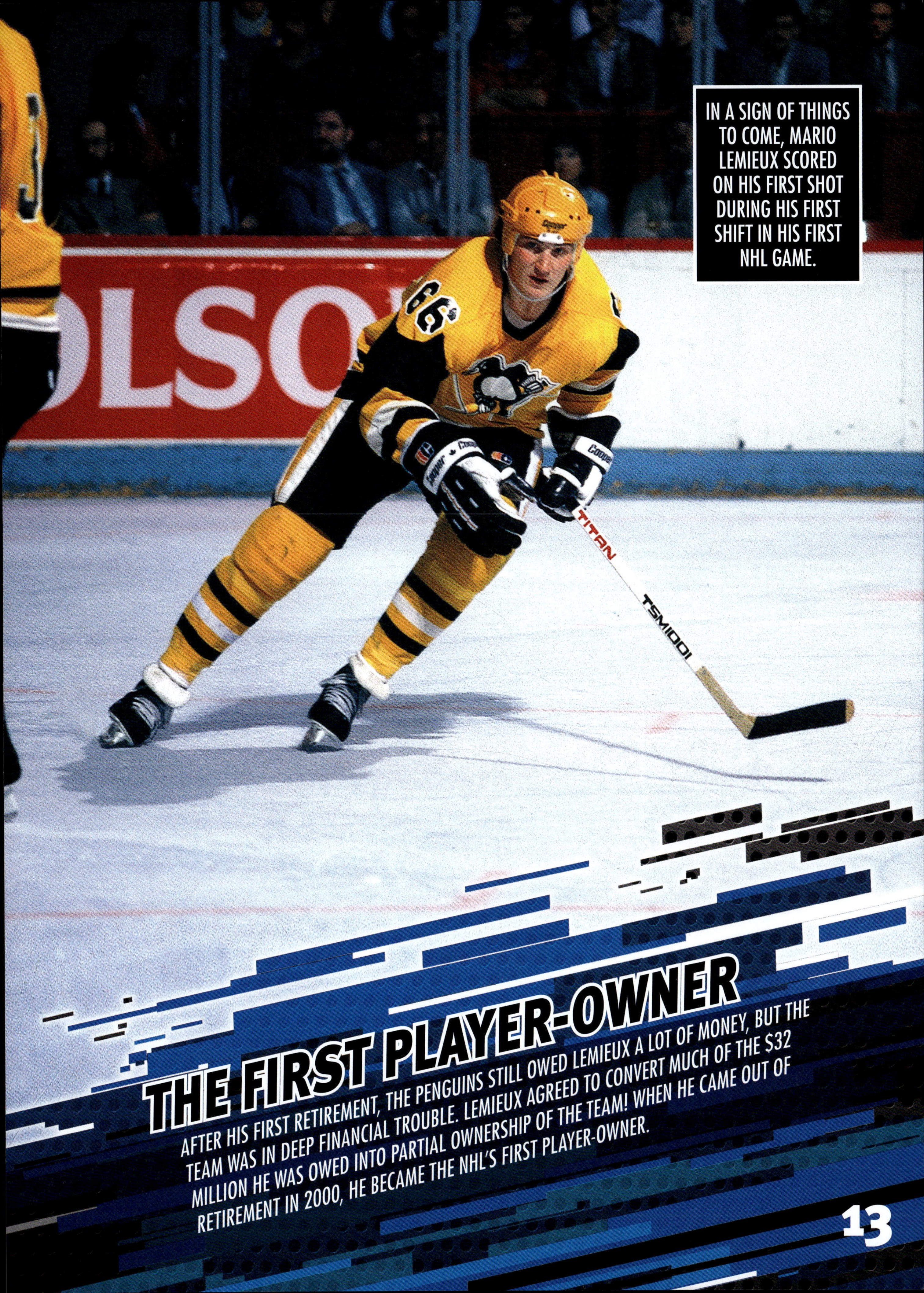

IN A SIGN OF THINGS TO COME, MARIO LEMIEUX SCORED ON HIS FIRST SHOT DURING HIS FIRST SHIFT IN HIS FIRST NHL GAME.

THE FIRST PLAYER-OWNER

AFTER HIS FIRST RETIREMENT, THE PENGUINS STILL OWED LEMIEUX A LOT OF MONEY, BUT THE TEAM WAS IN DEEP FINANCIAL TROUBLE. LEMIEUX AGREED TO CONVERT MUCH OF THE $32 MILLION HE WAS OWED INTO PARTIAL OWNERSHIP OF THE TEAM! WHEN HE CAME OUT OF RETIREMENT IN 2000, HE BECAME THE NHL'S FIRST PLAYER-OWNER.

THE GOLDEN JET

Bobby Hull was born in 1939 in Ontario, Canada, and played 15 seasons for the Chicago Blackhawks. Known for his hard shot, Hull scored 604 goals and led the NHL in scoring three times, which helped the Hawks win the Stanley Cup in 1961. His great speed and blond hair earned him the nickname "Golden Jet."

Bobby Hull and his son Brett were the first father/son pair to both score 50 goals in a season and have at least 600 goals and 1,000 points in their careers. They were also the first father and son to enter the Hockey Hall of Fame!

BOBBY HULL

BRETT HULL, SHOWN HERE IN HIS ST. LOUIS BLUES UNIFORM, SCORED THE WINNING GOAL TO WIN THE STANLEY CUP FOR DALLAS IN 1999.

THE GOLDEN BRETT

BRETT HULL WAS BORN IN 1964 IN ONTARIO, CANADA. HE PLAYED FOR FIVE DIFFERENT NHL TEAMS OVER 19 YEARS, INCLUDING 11 YEARS WITH ST. LOUIS. HE ONCE SCORED 86 GOALS IN ONE SEASON—THE THIRD-MOST EVER—AND HIS 741 CAREER GOALS ARE FOURTH ON THE ALL-TIME LIST. HE WON HIS SECOND STANLEY CUP WITH THE DETROIT RED WINGS IN 2002.

BOSTON'S BEST

Bobby Orr, born in 1948, in Ontario, Canada, played mostly for the Boston Bruins. Most people say he's the greatest defenseman ever because he changed the way the position was played. Before him, defenders just tried to keep the other team from scoring—but Orr himself was a great scorer, so it was like having an extra attacker. Sometimes he even led his team in scoring!

Orr played for Boston from 1966 to 1976 and led the Bruins to two Stanley Cups. However, he had to retire while he played for Chicago in 1979 because of knee **injuries**. He was only 30 years old.

BOBBY ORR WAS ONE OF THE FASTEST SKATERS IN THE NHL. HE SCORED THE GAME-WINNING GOAL IN OVERTIME AGAINST SAINT LOUIS IN 1970 THAT GAVE THE BRUINS THE STANLEY CUP.

BY THE NUMBERS

BOBBY ORR HAD 915 POINTS IN JUST 657 CAREER GAMES, A RECORD WHEN HE RETIRED. OTHERS WHO PLAYED LONGER HAVE PASSED HIM, AND HE'S NOW 11TH OVERALL IN CAREER POINTS SCORED. HE ONCE SCORED 46 GOALS IN A SEASON AND HAD 100 POINTS OR MORE SIX TIMES. HE WAS NAMED THE NHL'S BEST DEFENSEMAN A RECORD EIGHT TIMES!

GREAT DEFENDER

Some great players never get a Stanley Cup, and Ray Bourque was nearly one of them. Bourque was a defenseman drafted by the Boston Bruins in 1979. He was almost never hurt and was a smooth skater, excellent on both offense and defense.

He was named the NHL's best defenseman five times and his 410 goals and 1,579 points are the most ever by a defenseman. He scored 20 goals or more in a season nine times! However, during his time in Boston, the Bruins came close to winning the Stanley Cup but never quite got there—and that's what Bourque wanted most of all.

AFTER WAITING 22 YEARS, RAY BOURQUE FINALLY GOT TO LIFT THE STANLEY CUP IN 2001 WITH COLORADO AFTER THE AVALANCHE BEAT NEW JERSEY IN THE FINALS.

THE 22-YEAR WAIT

AFTER 20 YEARS WITH BOSTON AND NO STANLEY CUP, THE BRUINS WERE STRUGGLING AGAIN IN 2000. THEY OFFERED TO TRADE BOURQUE TO A DIFFERENT TEAM—ONE WITH A MUCH BETTER CHANCE OF WINNING. BOURQUE WENT TO THE COLORADO AVALANCHE. THEY WON THE CUP A YEAR LATER AND BOURQUE RETIRED AS A WINNER.

THE DEVIL INSIDE

Goalies might not (usually) score points, but they're very important players. Martin Brodeur was a goalie drafted by the New Jersey Devils in 1990. He was the NHL Rookie of the Year in 1994 and helped the Devils win their first Stanley Cup one year later. He led the Devils to two more Stanley Cup wins in 2000 and 2003 and eventually became the league's all-time leader in wins (691) before he retired in 2015.

Brodeur also played in the Olympics for Team Canada four times, winning gold in 2002 and 2010. He was inducted into the Hockey Hall of Fame in 2018.

MARTIN BRODEUR'S GOALTENDING STATS

* REGULAR SEASON GAMES PLAYED	1,266
* REGULAR SEASON WINS	691
* REGULAR SEASON SHUTOUTS	125
* 40-WIN SEASONS	8
REGULAR SEASON GOALS-AGAINST AVERAGE	2.24
PLAYOFF GAMES PLAYED	205
PLAYOFF WINS	113
* PLAYOFF SHUTOUTS	24
PLAYOFF GOALS-AGAINST AVERAGE	2.02
STANLEY CUP CHAMPIONSHIPS	3

* NHL RECORD

GUARDING THE NET

WHAT IF THE GREATEST HOCKEY PLAYER WASN'T SOMEONE WHO TRIED TO SCORE GOALS, BUT SOMEONE WHO TRIED TO STOP THEM? THAT'S WHAT GOALIES DO—STAND IN FRONT OF THEIR OWN NET. THEY WEAR SAFETY **EQUIPMENT** SO THEY DON'T GET HURT WHEN OTHER PLAYERS SHOOT PUCKS AT THEM—SOMETIMES AS FAST AS 100 MILES (161 KM) PER HOUR!

WHO IS THAT MASKED MAN?

Maybe the greatest player is the goalie who won the most championships! There are two of them. Montreal Canadiens goalies Jacques Plante and Ken Dryden both won six Stanley Cups.

Plante played 11 seasons with Montreal, from 1952 to 1963 and later played for New York, St. Louis, Toronto, and Boston. In 18 years, he won 437 games.

Goalies never wore masks before Plante did. He was hit in the face during a game in 1959 and had to get stitches. He came back into the game wearing the mask for protection and he never played without it again! Today, all goalies wear masks.

JACQUES PLANTE HOLDS ONE OF THE EARLIEST GOALIE MASKS. IT WASN'T MUCH, BUT IT CUT DOWN ON INJURIES AND OTHER GOALIES QUICKLY FOLLOWED SUIT.

NOT ONLY CAN YOU SEE DRYDEN'S MASK, BUT HERE HE IS MAKING A "KICK SAVE" WITH HIS LEG TO PREVENT ROD GILBERT OF THE NEW YORK RANGERS FROM SCORING.

HE'S A WINNER

KEN DRYDEN ONLY PLAYED IN EIGHT SEASONS FOR MONTREAL FROM 1970 TO 1979—BUT HE WAS A CHAMPION IN SIX OF THEM. HE WON 258 REGULAR SEASON GAMES, AND HIS 80 PLAYOFF VICTORIES ARE A TEAM RECORD. DRYDEN AND PLANTE SHARE THE TEAM'S PLAYOFF RECORD OF 10 SHUTOUTS.

THE BIG RED MACHINE

Men's ice hockey became an Olympic event in 1920. People from all around the world began to play it more! One of the most successful Olympic hockey programs came from the Soviet Union (now Russia). This team, nicknamed the Big Red Machine, won a medal in every Olympics from 1956 through 1988, including seven golds.

During much of that time, the Soviets had one of the greatest lines ever. It featured three of the best players of all time: Valery Kharlamov, Vladimir Petrov, and Boris Mikhailov. They played together in 207 games and combined for 448 goals between 1968 and 1980.

SOVIET PLAYERS VALERY KHARLAMOV (17), VLADIMIR PETROV (16), AND BORIS MIKHAILOV (13) FORMED ONE OF THE MOST SUCCESSFUL HOCKEY LINES EVER—BUT THEY COULDN'T BEAT TEAM USA IN 1980.

THE USA HOCKEY TEAM CELEBRATES WINNING AFTER DEFEATING FINLAND 4-2 IN THE GOLD MEDAL MATCH DURING THE 1980 OLYMPICS.

MIRACLE ON ICE

THE US MEN'S HOCKEY TEAM UPSET THE SOVIETS 4-3 IN THE OLYMPIC SEMIFINALS IN 1980. MADE UP OF YOUNG COLLEGE PLAYERS, THE AMERICAN TEAM STUNNED THE HEAVILY FAVORED TEAM FROM THE USSR IN A GAME THAT BECAME KNOWN AS THE MIRACLE ON ICE. GUIDED BY COACH HERB BROOKS, THE AMERICANS THEN BEAT FINLAND TO WIN THE GOLD.

WOMEN'S HOCKEY LEGEND

If you're wondering about the greatest female hockey player of all time, there's an easy answer. Hayley Wickenheiser was born August 12, 1978 in Saskatchewan, Canada. As a player, she led Team Canada to one silver and four gold medals in the Olympics, including twice as MVP. She's the all-time leader among Canadian women in Olympic goals (18), assists (33), and points (51). She also led Canada to seven gold and six silver medals at the Women's World Hockey Championships.

Wickenheiser retired in 2017 with 168 goals for Team Canada. She joined the Toronto Maple Leafs' player development team in 2018, helping them to find and train new talent.

HAYLEY WICKENHEISER HOLDS THE CANADIAN FLAG AFTER LEADING TEAM CANADA TO A GOLD MEDAL IN THE 2014 WINTER OLYMPICS. CANADA BEAT TEAM USA 3-2 IN OVERTIME IN THE CHAMPIONSHIP.

CAMMI GRANATO OF TEAM USA SHOOTS AGAINST SWEDEN DURING THE SALT LAKE CITY WINTER OLYMPIC GAMES IN 2002.

AMERICAN PIONEER

CAMMI GRANATO WAS A FOUNDING MEMBER OF THE US WOMEN'S NATIONAL TEAM. AS TEAM CAPTAIN, SHE LED THE AMERICANS TO A GOLD MEDAL IN THE 1998 OLYMPICS AND TO SILVER IN 2002. SHE SCORED 54 GOALS IN 54 GAMES FOR TEAM USA AND, IN 2010, BECAME THE FIRST WOMAN TO ENTER THE HOCKEY HALL OF FAME.

WHAT DO YOU THINK?

There are many other great players who could be on this list, such as Mark Messier, Stan Mikita, Steve Yzerman, Guy LaFleur, Jaromir Jagr, or Mike Bossy. All of these players were among the best in the world at the times in which they played.

There's no easy answer about who is the greatest hockey player of all time—if you ask 10 different people, you could get 10 different answers. It's **subjective**, and your own answer will depend on whom you like best. Who do *you* think is the greatest hockey player of all time?

YOU CAN LEARN ABOUT MORE HOCKEY GREATS AT THE HOCKEY HALL OF FAME IN TORONTO!

IF HE PLAYS LONG ENOUGH AND CAN STAY HEALTHY, WASHINGTON CAPITALS FORWARD ALEXANDER OVECHKIN HAS A CHANCE TO BREAK WAYNE GRETZKY'S CAREER GOAL-SCORING RECORD.

THE STARS OF TODAY

MAYBE THE GREATEST HOCKEY PLAYER OF ALL TIME IS PLAYING RIGHT NOW! THERE ARE MANY TALENTED AND EXCITING PLAYERS IN THE GAME RIGHT NOW, INCLUDING ALEXANDER OVECHKIN, SIDNEY CROSBY, CONNOR MCDAVID, STEVEN STAMKOS, AND PATRICK KANE. BY THE TIME THEY'RE FINISHED PLAYING, MAYBE ONE OF THEM WILL BE THE BEST!

GLOSSARY

cancer: a disease caused by the uncontrolled growth of cells in the body

draft: selecting a player from a group of potential players entering the league

equipment: tools, clothing, and other items needed for a job

foundation: a group supported by money given to them that does work that helps a community

hat trick: in hockey, when three goals are scored by one player in a game

injury: harm or damage

inscribe: to cut words into a surface

penalty: a punishment for breaking a rule

retirement: the act of ending your working career

rookie: a player who is in their first year in the league

subjective: based on your personal feelings

suspend: to stop from playing a sport for a time

waive: to get rid of a requirement

FOR MORE INFORMATION

BOOKS

Romanuk, Paul. *Hockey Superstars Series.* Toronto, Ontario, Canada: Scholastic Canada Ltd, 2019.

Sports Illustrated Kids. *Face-Off: Top 10 Lists of Everything in Hockey (Sports Illustrated Kids Top 10 Lists).* New York, NY: Sports Illustrated Kids, 2015.

Sports Illustrated Kids. *Hockey: Then to WOW!* New York, NY: Sports Illustrated Kids, 2017.

WEBSITES

Hockey: Learn All About the Sport of Hockey
www.ducksters.com/sports/hockey.php
Learn all about hockey on this kid-friendly website.

NHL.com
www.nhl.com/fans/nhl-centennial/100-greatest-nhl-players
The NHL's official website lists its choices for the top 100 players.

Ranker
www.ranker.com/list/famous-female-ice-hockey-players/reference
The site lists its choices for the top women's hockey players.

Publisher's note to educators and parents: Our editors have carefully reviewed these websites to ensure that they are suitable for students. Many websites change frequently, however, and we cannot guarantee that a site's future contents will continue to meet our high standards of quality and educational value. Be advised that students should be closely supervised whenever they access the internet.

INDEX

GREATEST OF ALL TIME SPORTS STARS

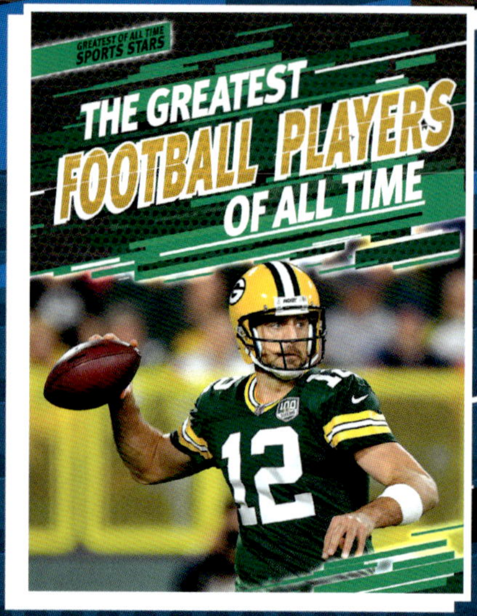

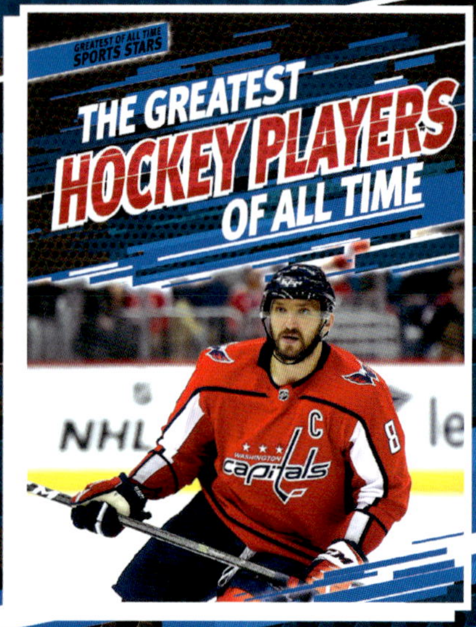

Gareth Stevens PUBLISHING

ISBN: 9781538247839
6-pack ISBN: 9781538247846
9 781538 247839